The Undercover Kids' Holland Adventure

THE TRUNK
IN THE ATTIC

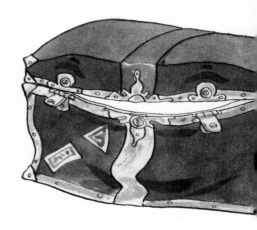

Madurodam
The Hague

Scheveningen
Amsterdam
The Hague
Rotterdam

Gevangenpoort
The Hague

GERMANY

BELGIUM

Follow Katie, Jake, Dirk and Cooper as they bicycle through Holland. They enjoy great food, have fun on the beach and meet their Great-Grandpa's friend, Madame van den Berg.

The Undercover Kids' Holland Adventure

THE T
IN THE

RUNK
ATTIC

By **GLORIA SMITH ZAWASKI**
with illustrations
by **KAREN DONNELLY**

THE EXCITING READ PUBLISHING GROUP NEWBURGH, NEW YORK

This edition first published
in the United States of America
in 2009 by The Exciting Read Publishing Group
174 South St, Newburgh, NY 12550

Test your knowledge
about the Undercover Kids adventure
and the faraway lands they visit.
Go to www.TheUndercoverKids.com.

Summary: Katie and Jake are two city kids who
are visiting their aunt's farm in Ulster County, New York
for the summer. They explore the farmhouse and
discover a small room with a very old trunk.
The purple wristbands in the trunk lead them
to an underground tunnel on Aunt Jean's Farm
and the fun begins.

Book design by Phillip Ritzenberg

Printed in the United States of America

ISBN -13: 978-1-935373-00-1 ISBN -10: 1-935373-00-5

Edition
10 9 8 7 6 5 4 3 2 1

Are you ready for the challenge?

Katie, Jake and Cooper travel
In underground tunnels
And through time.

That's how they get
All the way to Holland.
Sometimes it only takes a day
To change a lifetime.

If you're up for an adventure,
Travel with them.
There's a whole world waiting
To be discovered.

Got your purple bracelet?
Then it's time to turn the page.
Are you ready? Let's go!

This book belongs to:

_____

An Undercover Kid

Greenland

Dirk
in
Amsterdam

Katie, Jake
and Cooper
in
New York

Africa

South
America

Asia

Europe — the next
Undercover Kids
adventure.
MONGOLIA

Middle East

Australia

In this, their first adventure, Katie, Jake and Cooper travel from New York to Holland. Look for their next adventure which takes them to Mongolia.

CONTENTS

Meet the Undercover Kids
Katie, Jake and their dog, Cooper,

KATIE

Confident and responsible, Katie likes looking out for Jake, and even Cooper–most of the time, that is.

JAKE

Jake's not always sure of himself, but he sure can solve a lot of things.

COOPER

There aren't many dogs like Cooper, and that's okay with him!

...their family
and the talking trunk,

GREAT-GRANDPA

Great-Grandpa Henry had the Wanderlust and loved journeying beyond the horizon.

AUNT JEAN

It's hard to imagine Aunt Jean anywhere but on her farm.

THE TRUNK

The trunk is old, wise and funny, too.

...and their Dutch friends.
Well, it's true, they're not all friends.

DIRK

Dirk seems older than his years. He has traveled undercover a long time.

MADAME

When you're with Madame van den Berg you want to stay and listen to her stories.

THE WAITER

The waiter would like to be very rich–one way or another.

"If you want to meet people different from you,
I've got a suggestion—here's what you should do:
Travel to other countries—it's a wonderful way
To meet new people and have a great day.

There are kids the world over, just like you.
Why don't you become an Undercover Kid, too?
All you'll need is a purple band
To whisk you away to faraway lands."

THE TRUNK IN THE ATTIC

CHAPTER ONE

Summer Vacation

KATIE AND JAKE live in New York City, except during the summer and winter vacations, when they visit Aunt Jean's farm. They have been going there for as long as they can remember.

Their parents are professors. Mom teaches languages and speaks quite a few. Dad is an archaeologist and spends summers in foreign countries digging for things. He uncovers old bones and pieces of old pots. Mom learns about the culture, especially the languages. Someday, they say, Katie and Jake can come, too. Katie is ten and Jake is seven. Maybe "someday" isn't too far away.

Aunt Jean is Dad's sister, but to Katie and Jake they seem totally different. Dad loves having people around, traveling and living in the city. He insists on keeping things neat, and everything has a place in their apartment.

Aunt Jean doesn't spend a lot of time cleaning—just tidying up. She never leaves the farm unless there is a good reason. Her hair is long and black with streaks of gray, and Katie likes to

It was hard for Katie and Jake to imagine that all the people in these portraits were their relatives.

watch her put it up in lots of different ways.

In the summer, Aunt Jean always wears blue jeans and t-shirts. During the cold winter, she keeps warm with faded flannel shirts. Aunt Jean has favorite things—favorite jeans, a favorite denim shirt and a favorite worn-out sweater.

Aunt Jean lives on the farm alone, but she says she is never lonely. She has four cats, two old horses no one rides anymore, a grouchy goat, and an assortment of noisy chickens, guinea hens, geese and ducks.

The farm has been in the family for almost two hundred years. Aunt Jean jokes that she sometimes feels like she lives with all their ancestors. Family portraits hang on most of the walls of the farmhouse.

Katie and Jake think that most of the people in the portraits look stern in their fancy black clothes. It's hard for Katie to imagine they are all her relatives because she never likes to put on dress-up clothes.

There is one portrait that they really like to look at—the photograph on the mantel of Great-Grandpa Henry. He has red hair, a red beard, blue eyes, and, unlike their other ancestors, a big, wide, smile that makes you want to smile back.

Katie and Jake never knew their great-grandparents on their father's side of the family. Great-Grandpa Henry died long before they were born, and Great-Grandma Sarah died even before he did.

Aunt Jean says Great-Grandpa Henry had the "Wanderlust." He loved to travel anywhere he could, any chance he could. He traveled by canoe, kayak, boats, airplanes and the railroad. In the barn are remnants of Great-Grandpa Henry's travels—everything from old pictures of his days as a pilot during World War II to the rickety, old biplane and canoe. Old car parts are everywhere.

In back of the barn is the widest, deepest hole that Katie and Jake have ever seen. Great-Grandpa Henry started digging it years and years ago when he was a kid. Aunt Jean says it was for silage, or feed, for the cows, but Dad says Great-Grandpa Henry thought that he was going to reach China.

When Katie and Jake were younger, they dug the hole just like Great-Grandpa. Each year they spent hours digging in the pit, with their dog Cooper enthusiastically helping out. They imagined what it would be like to reach China and other foreign lands as they dug.

Though the hole never got much deeper, Katie and Jake found lots of rocks and fossils and even an old penny from 1859.

Aunt Jean said the penny was made just before the Civil War and that it was probably worth a lot of money, although it should never be sold. "The real value in things is what they mean to you," she said. "This penny may have come from one of our relatives long ago."

Aunt Jean said that Great-Grandpa Henry finally got to China on a steamship. She said that Katie and Jake must carry the wanderlust gene as well. Maybe someday they'd reach China, too.

Now only Cooper continues the tradition of digging.

Dad says that Cooper is the kind of dog that is an "all kinds" dog, but mainly the kind of dog they should never have brought home from the animal shelter. Still everybody, even Dad, loves Cooper.

Dad thinks Cooper has far too much energy for the apartment. Every day they'd take Cooper to the fenced-in dog run in the park to play with other dogs. He always ended up digging by the fence. He wanted to get free to run through the

In the barn, Katie and Jake find everything from old pictures of Great-Grandpa Henry's to the rickety, old biplane and canoe.

park. That's why he was always on a leash.

On the farm, Cooper could run loose if Katie and Jake would keep an eye on him. When Cooper digs, he is busy, so he can be trusted to stay on the farm. Was he trying to get to China, or was he hoping to unearth a bone? No one is sure except Cooper himself.

Cooper is a picture of dogged determination.

CHAPTER TWO

Up From the Underground

ONE COOL SUMMER day, Katie and Jake were swinging on the old rope from the barn rafters when they heard Cooper barking furiously. They ran to find Cooper. As they approached the pit, they found Cooper running around and around in circles at the bottom.

They slid down the bank of dried dirt and clay where they saw that Cooper had unearthed a big, wide, round cover—it looked like the manhole covers they stepped on and over a million times in New York City. It had an old handle. Jake was reaching to pull on it when suddenly the cover started rising all by itself. Katie and Jake stumbled backward out of the way.

They watched as a boy climbed out of what looked like a bottomless pit.

He had sparkling blue eyes and blonde hair. Katie figured he must be at least 12 years old. He was a little taller than Katie, but something about him seemed older.

"I saw a light," he said. "But this entrance has

been closed off for years." Cooper kept barking, but at a distance. Katie and Jake stood frozen by fright—and intense curiosity.

"Hi! I'm Dirk." The boy reached out to shake their hands, and Katie and Jake noticed a bright, purple band on his left wrist. Cooper barked and sniffed, and barked and sniffed some more. Then, satisfied that the intruder meant no harm, he sat down.

"I'm on my way back to Holland. Did you come to show me around? I'd like to see this part of America, but I don't have time to visit this time. I'm on my way home. Coming with me?"

"C-c-c-oming with you?" Katie stuttered. She wanted to look past Dirk and see into the hole, but she didn't want to get too close.

Dirk looked around at all the dirt. Next he stared at their wrists. Then he backed away toward the tunnel.

"Wait," said Katie. "What's wrong?"

"No, it's okay...I've gotta get going." Dirk looked around nervously.

"Don't go...you just got here. I mean, it isn't every day someone just drops in or, er... pops up... out of nowhere," Katie said.

"Yeah, we thought Cooper was digging for

Katie and Jake watched as a boy climbed out of what looked like a bottomless pit.

China…not for, well…people," Jake chimed in.

Cooper was on guard, not certain what the problem was but sensing there must be a problem somewhere.

"Digging for China?" Dirk asked.

"It's a family thing," Katie replied. "We used to dig and imagine that we would find faraway lands. Cooper just digs to dig."

"But you're not…Undercover Kids?"

"What's an undercover kid?" Jake asked, wanting to become one, whatever it meant.

"There must have been one here sometime. Otherwise why would there be a cover?" Dirk said.

And with that, he backed up. "If you ever get a band, come to Holland. I'll be waiting." Then he jumped back in the hole. The cover shut and clamped tight. He was gone.

Just then Aunt Jean called out from a distance, "Katie! Jake! Where are you?" Katie threw dirt over the cover. "This is our secret," she whispered to Jake. "Don't say a word." And with that she grabbed Jake's pinky and hooked it with hers. "I swear," he replied.

Jake wished he could tell Aunt Jean everything, but he wanted Katie's approval and trust more than anything else in the world.

They ran to meet Aunt Jean as Cooper circled her, barking. "What's all the commotion?" she asked.

"Cooper saw a rabbit," Katie said, giving Jake a look that said he shouldn't say anything different.

"I'm hungry, Aunt Jean," said Jake as he grabbed her hand.

Katie wasn't sure if Jake was really hungry or if he was better at keeping a secret than she'd imagined.

Back at the farmhouse, they took off their dirty shoes and walked in socks on the wide wood floor boards. Aunt Jean had dinner waiting—soup with vegetables from the garden was cooking in a big, black kettle that sat on the woodstove. The corn bread in the iron skillet shaped like an ear of corn was sweet and warm enough to have the butter melt right into it. Katie didn't realize just how hungry she was.

CHAPTER THREE

The Voice in the Attic

AFTER DINNER Katie and Jake were tired. They went upstairs to their rooms, which were up a set of narrow, steep stairs that Aunt Jean didn't like to climb much anymore. Aunt Jean's room was on the first floor.

Jake at first felt strange and a little afraid that his room was so far from Aunt Jean's, but now he was used to his farm bedroom. It was small with an old iron bed frame that made creaky noises when Jake sat on it.

Katie was in a room next to Jake's. Her bed was bigger than his and had a quilt made of colorful squares that Aunt Jean had made. The bed was in a corner of the room, right under the place where the slanted roof met the floor.

Katie had to scoot to the outside of the bed when she sat up. She loved curling up to sleep on the inside, right under the roof where everything felt safe and cozy.

There was an attic on the third floor up a rickety, old staircase. The attic contained "stuff."

Stuff that had been there since the house was built. Aunt Jean called the attic a nightmare and said every house has a room that's filled with stuff you just can't throw out.

Katie and Jake's apartment in New York City did not have a "stuff" room. Mom gave away their old clothes and other things they no longer needed to the Salvation Army. There wasn't room for stuff or "clutter" as their mom called it.

Years ago Katie had dared Jake to go up into Aunt Jean's attic. They both peeked in.

Everything looked old, dark and scary. They never dared go back again.

Jake was glad that Mom packed his winter pajamas for his summer vacation. He liked the flannel because it's soft inside.

He got in bed and thought about his parents on their trip to Mexico. He didn't know for certain where Mexico was, but he knew it was far away. He remembered the waiters in big sombrero hats at the Mexican restaurant in New York City near their apartment.

"Why would Mom and Dad want to go to Mexico?" Jake asked as he climbed onto Katie's bed.

"Because it's fun to see different countries and

see how different people live," said Katie as she pulled the covers over the headboard so it surrounded them like a tent.

"Why can't they see how different people live right here?" Jake asked, thinking about the waiters and wondering if everyone in Mexico wore hats like that.

"Because you don't really know people from other countries until you see them in their own country," Katie explained.

"At least that's what Mom says. I can't wait to go to other countries. There are lots of them, you know. More than you can count. There are even more countries than there are states in America," Katie said. "Holland is in the Netherlands. That's where Dirk's from."

"But how did he get here?" Jake asked. "What's under that cover? A subway?"

"Not all the way out here!" Katie laughed.

Suddenly they heard another voice. They froze, afraid to pull back their tent-sheets.

> *If you want to meet people different*
> *from you,*
> *I've got a suggestion—here's what*
> *you should do:*

Katie and Jake heard another voice. They froze, afraid to pull back their tent-sheets.

Travel to other countries—it's a
*   wonderful way*
To meet new people and have a great day.

"Stop trying to scare me," Jake whispered loudly to Katie. Jake couldn't see Katie's face. If he could, he'd have known that the deep voice didn't come from her.

There are kids the world over, just
*   like you.*
Why don't you become Undercover
*   Kids, too?*
All you'll need are purple bands
To whisk you away to faraway lands.

The attic. The voice was coming from the attic Katie realized.

Katie whispered to Jake: "Jake, promise you won't say anything about this to anyone, not even Aunt Jean. I think the voice is about Dirk...and the cover. If we tell, we'll spoil it. We can handle this ourselves."

Jake was afraid, but not afraid enough to go against Katie. "I swear," he said, and once again locked little fingers with Katie. He wished he could crawl into bed with Aunt Jean or maybe go to Mexico with Mom and Dad.

"Okay, Cooper, they're upstairs." It was Aunt Jean's voice. She had taken Cooper out for his evening walk, and he was bounding up the stairs to be with them.

In a mere second, Cooper was between them in the bed, wrecking their tent.

Cooper wiggled this way and that. He knew he was lucky to be on the bed and not on his pad on the floor.

Soon Katie and Jake were curled up small like Cooper. They knew that Cooper would bark if anyone came into the room. Sleep conquered even their worst fears.

Now it was all quiet at the farmhouse except for the crickets outside.

The next morning Jake tumbled over Cooper and begged Katie to come downstairs to the bathroom with him.

"I've been holding all night!" he said, jumping from one foot to another doing the "potty dance." Katie went downstairs, and Cooper scrambled after them.

Katie stood outside the bathroom waiting her turn. Cooper ran in circles, eager to go out. Katie opened the back door, flipped up the hook on the screen door and then looked for Cooper's leash.

What happened next was a blur. Jake opened the bathroom door. Katie was about to go in the bathroom when Cooper took a flying leap out the screen door. He ran across the yard, disappeared in back of the barn and was gone.

The screen door slammed shut, waking Aunt Jean and all the barnyard animals. Katie ran from the bathroom and stepped out the kitchen door, but she couldn't get far with her bare feet on the gravely driveway. Besides, she'd never catch him. Why couldn't he learn to listen? Why couldn't he just stay?

"I guess Cooper has the wanderlust, too," said Aunt Jean with sleep still in her voice. "Help yourselves to cereal. I'll take the car and drive around to see if I can find him. Cooper would have to go pretty far and get fairly unlucky to meet up with a car at this time of the morning."

CHAPTER FOUR

The Purple Band Connection

WITH AUNT JEAN gone, Katie figured there would be time, but not a lot of time, to go up to the attic. She was certain that the voice had come from there.

In the daylight the idea of going into the attic seemed far less scary. Besides, she wasn't worried about Cooper. She knew he'd come back when he was good and ready.

Jake was far more interested in cereal, even Aunt Jean's kind of no-sugar cereal, than what was in the attic, but he followed Katie up the stairs anyway.

As Katie pulled open the door, it creaked on worn-out hinges.

It was hard to breathe inside. Light came from the one attic window which was dirty and covered with cobwebs. They tiptoed carefully along the beams.

The attic had no real floor, just old beams with insulation stuffed in between. Here and there pieces of plywood were laid across the beams to

support boxes, piles of old books and magazines, and a rack for old clothes wrapped in plastic covers with zippers.

In the center of the room was a big, old trunk. It must have been black at one time, but now it was dusty and gray. Great-Grandpa's name— Henry Anderson—was written on top.

Katie reached for the trunk. What if the voice came from inside? Fearful, she pulled her hand back. She counted to three, then reached for the trunk again.

"AH...AH...AH...AH...CHOOO," said the trunk. It was the longest, loudest sneeze Katie and Jake had ever heard.

At first she thought the trunk was just hard to open. Then she saw that it was locked.

"We'll never find the key!" exclaimed Katie, looking around at all the stuff in the attic.

Jake thought that wasn't such bad news.

Katie spied a metal chest the size of a really big lunch box. She opened it and found all sorts of tools and nails and hardware inside. "Let's use this in the lock," she said to Jake, showing him the screwdriver.

Katie lifted the small cover over the keyhole,

then poked the screwdriver firmly inside. The trunk twisted and turned and lifted up into the air and suddenly the lid flew open.

"AH...AH...AH...AH...CHOOO!!"

It was the longest, loudest sneeze they'd ever heard.

The trunk slammed shut and ever-so-slowly began to open again.

> *Katie and Jake, do you suppose*
> *You could refrain from sticking objects*
>   *up my nose*

Then the trunk let out a big, long yawn.

"How do you know our names?" Katie asked in a shaky voice.

> *Do you mind if I don't answer in rhyme?*
> *It gets annoying to do it all the time.*

Hearing nothing from Katie and Jake, he continued.

"I know everything about everyone in this house. Since my traveling days ended over 50 years ago, I haven't much else to do but keep track of what goes on in the house and the barn."

"And behind the barn, too?" Katie asked.

The lid creaked, and the trunk let out a yelp. "Oh, ow! I've been closed so long, I think I've developed lockjaw. Give me a moment and let me stretch open."

The lid opened a little at first, then a lot...until in the dim light they saw what looked like a treasure chest of stuff inside. Katie and Jake came closer.

The trunk stayed open, so they came even closer. Finally, Katie reached in to see what she could find, but it was hard to see what was what.

Katie pulled her hand away in the nick of time as the lid suddenly slammed shut again.

"HA HA! HO HO! That tickled!" howled the trunk, startling Katie and Jake. The rafters shook as the trunk laughed.

Katie decided that with a little more light, maybe she could avoid tickling the trunk.

There was no light switch in the attic. There was a string dangling from a bulb in the ceiling above, but it was out of their reach. Katie stood on the lid of the trunk and reached the string.

"You're heavier than you look," said the trunk when she climbed off and the trunk opened its lid again.

They began pulling things out of the trunk and held them up to the light.

You haven't got all day, so may I suggest
You take what you need from inside
  my chest.
There are tunnels in countries everywhere.
The purple bands will help get you there.

Just think of the country you want to see
And the bands will get you there safely.
Enjoy! Explore! There's a whole world
  to discover.
Remember: You get just one day after
  going under the cover.

Then to get back home you will need
To have accomplished just one good deed.

Katie found a scarf and a picture in an old
tin frame.
The trunk smiled.

Those belonged to someone Henry knew.
He'd be glad you're taking them along
  with you.
It should be easy to find the woman.
Just show Cooper the scarf—let him take
  a whiff.

Jake grabbed medals on a chain.

Those are dog tags—they'll be your
  good fairy.
Henry got them while in the military.

There were some old coins.

Don't count on them.
Don't even try
To use them in stores.
There's not much they'll buy.

"Look at these," laughed Jake as he put on wire-framed glasses.

Look through them if you need to find
Something you ought not to leave behind.

And then they found a box—a wooden box with carving on its side. Katie picked it up, feeling that it held something very special. Jake looked over her shoulder as she opened it. There were two purple bands inside— the most beautiful deep purple she'd ever seen.

"That's the band that Dirk was wearing!!!" Jake exclaimed.

The lid slammed closed. "Geez, don't scare me like that," said the trunk. "I see you found them. Now listen closely. This is important, but I'm going to say this only one time," the trunk sighed, "in rhyme."

Not everyone is like you.
Some may be jealous of what your
*   bracelets can do.*

So keep them a secret, hide them well.
Don't show them to strangers.
If they ask, don't tell.

Katie and Jake heard the sound of tires on the dirt driveway. They hurried to the attic door when the trunk spoke again.

Why is it that even kids who are bright
Never remember to turn out the light?

The lid slammed shut, and this time Jake stood on the trunk and pulled the string. The trunk groaned but stood its ground.

Katie pulled the attic door open, and they both hurried down the rickety staircase. Before going downstairs they hid what they'd taken from the trunk under Katie's bed.

"Katie! Jake! I found him!" It was Aunt Jean calling from the driveway. Katie and Jake scampered down to the kitchen table as they caught their breath.

"Let's have more cereal," said Katie, as she quickly dumped cereal into their bowls so Aunt Jean wouldn't notice that they hadn't eaten since she'd left.

"Where was he?" Jake asked.

"Right here. When I drove up he was right on

the back porch. But he must have gone somewhere and met someone."

There on Cooper's neck was a purple collar just like the colored bands in the box under Katie's bed.

CHAPTER FIVE

Tunnel Travel

IT SEEMED TO TAKE forever to do the break-
fast dishes and wait for Aunt Jean's friends to
come. Ladies from the neighborhood were coming to make a "friendship quilt."

They gathered every so often and sewed all
afternoon, staying until dinnertime, cutting cloth,
laughing and swapping stories.

They finally arrived. Katie and Jake were
greeted by all four women. Some thought they'd
gotten bigger in the few weeks they'd been on the
farm. One commented that Jake had even more
freckles. Jake wished she hadn't said that.

Once the greetings were over, no one seemed
to notice when Katie and Jake went outside to
play, carrying a backpack filled with their new-
found treasures.

They went to the barn's first stall. There was
still some old, musty hay on the floor. They spread
out the things they'd taken from the box.

Remembering the trunk's instructions, Katie
held up the scarf so Cooper could take a long
sniff. He sniffed but wasn't the least bit interested.
Jake put on the glasses but didn't see any more

than he saw without them.

Katie pulled the carved box out of her back-pack. The purple wristbands seemed to glow against the red velvet on the bottom of the box. "Put your hand out," she instructed Jake. She slipped one band on her wrist first, then put the other on Jake's.

"Now repeat after me: I," said Katie.

"I," Jake repeated.

"Say your name," said Katie, as she said hers.

"Say your name, Katie," Jake repeated.

They were drawn by a force they could feel but not see, straight through a dark tunnel.

"Don't say 'Say your name.' Just say your name, Jake!" Katie was losing patience. "Never mind. Just say, 'Officially I'm now an Undercover Kid, and I want to go to Holland, and I vow to keep our bracelets a secret unless we're talking to other Undercover Kids.'"

"Do I have to say all that?" Jake asked.

Their bands began to glow, and they knew a connection to something powerful had been made. A surge pushed through their bodies from their head to their toes and out their fingertips. Even

Cooper sat up at attention.

Without a word between them, they walked toward the pit. Cooper walked close to them even without his leash.

When they reached the pit they saw the lid that Dirk had emerged from was open, but he was nowhere in sight. Cooper jumped right in.

That gave Katie and Jake confidence, and they followed right behind, down a small set of stairs that led to a dark room lit only by the sunlight peaking through the cover. Cooper was waiting at attention.

It took a moment for their eyes to adjust to the dark.

They faced two large doors. In an instant the doors opened, and they were off in a "whoosh" without a moment to think about turning back.

They were drawn by a force they could feel but not see, straight through a dark tunnel. Dim images sparkled on the ceiling of the tunnel: old sailing ships, paintings, windmills and flowers in every size, shape and color.

Ahead, Katie saw Cooper facing forward like the statues on the bows of old sailing ships, except his ears were flying out to the side. She and Jake felt like superheroes surfing on air.

Cooper didn't bark. Katie didn't speak. Jake didn't cry.

Then everything stopped. They scrambled onto a landing where there were two more doors. The doors swung open as they approached, and they saw a light coming through a hole above them.

There was a steep stairway that looked like a cross between a ladder and stairs.

"Do you think we did it? Do you think this is Holland?" asked Jake. His voice echoed.

They wanted to get out of the tunnel, but where were they?

Katie put Cooper's front paws on the ladder. She and Cooper were both a little unsteady, but Cooper finally managed to climb up the skinny stairs.

They found themselves in a small room—and there was Dirk. He was rolling up a rug that had hidden the cover on the floor.

"I knew you were coming," he said.

"How did you know?" Katie and Jake asked in unison.

"I just had a feeling from my bracelet, so I thought I'd check. First trips aren't always easy. Are you okay?" he asked.

They found themselves in a small room, and there was Dirk rolling up a rug that hid the cover on the floor.

Katie brushed herself off but then realized she wasn't a bit dirty. "Where are we?" she asked.

"Welkom to Amsterdam!" said Dirk, using a "v" sound at the beginning of the word.

"I thought we were going to Holland," said Jake.

"Amsterdam is the capital of Holland," Dirk explained.

"Is this somebody's room?" said Jake, wondering where exactly they were. Somehow it didn't seem like a real room to him.

"This is Anne Frank's attic. It's now a museum. People come here to remember her," Dirk explained.

"I know about her. I read her book," said Katie. "Is this the real place?"

"Yes," said Dirk.

"Who's Anne Frank?" Jake asked.

"Anne Frank was a Jewish girl who lived during World War II. She hid here for two years with her family because German solidiers were capturing Jews in Holland," said Dirk.

"What happened to her?" asked Jake with wide eyes.

"When Anne Frank and her family were discovered by the solidiers, they were sent off to a prison camp. She died there," Katie said.

"She did?" asked Jake. He didn't like anything with a scary ending.

"But it wasn't completely a sad story," Dirk explained. "A lot of people helped them."

"Helped them how?" Jake wanted to know.

"Well," Dirk thought for a moment. "In school we learned that a Dutch underground newspaper printed and handed out 30,000 stars to help support the Jews which said, 'Jews and non-Jews are one and the same'."

"Why didn't they just fight for them," asked Jake.

"The Germans were stronger," Dirk explained

"Besides, fighting doesn't always get you what you want," Katie added. "Sometimes you win by having a smart plan."

Cooper had enough of all this talk. He wanted to go out. Now.

CHAPTER SIX

Bikes, Bikes Everywhere

THEY HAD TO GO down another set of very steep steps—only they discovered that it was harder going down steps like this than going up. Cooper managed very well, probably because he was so eager to go out.

"This is a canal house," Dirk explained. "We have a lot of people in Holland but not a lot of land. So we build skinny houses, like this one, that are very tall and very steep.

Dirk pointed to the big hooks at the top of many of the canal houses. "We use those pulleys to hoist big things, like furniture, through the windows," he says. "Some things are too big to carry up those steep, narrow stairs."

"They look like the brownstone houses near where we live in New York City," said Jake.

Dirk laughed. "A lot of Dutch people went to live in New York City. It used to be called New Amsterdam," he said. "You know the Hudson River? That's named after Henry Hudson. He sailed to America for the Dutch."

"So the brownstones were built by Dutch people?" Jake asked.

"Ja," said Dirk. "The idea to build like that came from Dutch people."

Cooper had a where-am-I look on his face and was eager to begin exploring. There were lots of bicycles parked here, there and everywhere. Dirk pointed to three of the bicycles and said, "Climb aboard."

Katie and Jake were wary of the bikes. They had ridden bikes at home but not a lot. It was dangerous in the city, and, at Aunt Jean's, the driveway was rocky and the roads really hilly. Besides, the old bikes she had in the shed had flat tires.

"You are going to enjoy riding bikes here because our country is flat. Holland used to be under the sea," explained Dirk.

"What do you mean, 'It used to be under the sea'?" asked Jake.

"It's land that we got by pushing back the sea with big dams we call dikes," explained Dirk.

"Oh, right. Once one sprang a leak, and a kid put his finger in the hole," said Jake. "I know that story."

"It's not true. But everyone tells that story," said Dirk.

Dirk had keys for the bikes, and he took a minute to make sure everyone's seat was adjusted. "We have lots of extra bikes for visitors here," he said.

Each bike had a basket in front. Dirk put Cooper in his basket. Their backpack went into Katie's. Then they were off.

At first Katie and Jake felt a bit wobbly, but the bikes were sturdy, and it didn't take much to keep their balance. They pedaled along with lots and lots of other people on bikes. They had never seen so many.

Once in a while a bike wheel would get stuck inside a tram track on the road. The trams looked like subways attached to overhead wires. Just like puppets on a string, Katie thought.

Jake liked stopping on the arched bridges that went across the canals. He waved to the sightseeing boats going under the bridges.

Katie loved the flower market. Everything was displayed on boats. There were flowers of every kind in every color. She didn't think she had ever seen so many beautiful flowers all in one place.

"This is our Bloemenmarkt," Dirk said. "It's the only floating flower market in the world. People in Holland are great gardeners.

We ship flower bulbs, like tulips and daffodils, all over the world."

They walked alongside the market, and Jake laughed every time people spoke. "It sounds like they're all clearing their throats," Jake said.

"Jake. That's rude," said Katie.

But Dirk just laughed. "It's true. Many of our sounds come from way back in our throats."

"I'm sooo hungry," Jake complained. Katie realized she was hungry, too. Cooper was licking his lips. Dirk came to a halt in front of a sign that

Jake waved to the sightseeing boats going under the bridges. Katie loved the floating flower market

read "Poffertjeskraam."

Katie tried to sound it out: "Poff-ert-jez-kram." It was hard to say but fun to try.

They slipped a lock through the wheels of their bikes and went inside. Cooper trotted alongside them, and no one seemed to care.

"Dogs are like people in Holland," Dirk said.

Outside on the porch, they sat at a table where they could watch the cook. He was busy pouring batter into a heavy-looking black pan with a lot of little indentations for the batter. They breathed in the smell of baking butter as if that alone would satisfy their hunger.

The *poffertjes* puffed up to be round on top, about the size of a golf ball. "Spreekt u Engels?" asked the man as he flipped about ten on to each of their plates. Just before they dug in he covered the *poffertjes* with butter and powdered sugar.

"Yes, we're American," answered Katie. Then she wondered if she should have told him that.

Katie and Jake couldn't remember ever eating anything so good. Dirk paid the check in bills he called "euros." "I work at my uncle's tailor shop to earn extra money. A very big part of the money I earn goes here," he said with a smile.

"I think I love Dutch food," said Katie as they unlocked their bikes.

She put her backpack in the basket, and Dirk hoisted Cooper into his. Dirk said Cooper felt lots heavier. Katie guessed Cooper found a few sugary *poffertjes* under the table.

CHAPTER SEVEN

Tiny Buildings and Big Ships

I T WAS JUST about 11 AM. Dirk thought about the day ahead. There was so much to show them.

Dirk suggested they travel by train. They could put their bikes on the train and pay for a one-day ticket that would let them get on and off at different stops. "Lots of stops, just one ticket," Dirk said.

Katie apologized that they hadn't brought any money with them. "Don't worry," said Dirk. Then Jake reminded her of the coins from the trunk. Katie reached in the backpack, pulled out the coins and handed them to Dirk.

He looked at them carefully. "They're mainly from England, but some are from Holland. Look, they're all dated from the 1940s. I'd like to add these to my coin collection, if you don't mind. Then we'll be even."

Kate and Jake nodded gratefully.

Their first stop is Madurodam—a entire tiny city of little buildings that is like a miniature city

Katie and Jake felt like giants in the city of tiny buildings at Madurodam.

in the Netherlands. Katie and Jake felt like giants.
There were four kilometers of train tracks.
Everywhere were miniature buildings and cars.
The trains ran on miniature tracks, doors to some
of the buildings opened and closed, and the wind-
mill blades moved.

Katie and Jake were as excited as they had
been the first time they saw an elaborate train set
at FAO Schwartz.

One place was a clog factory where, in
exchange for a euro, Dirk bought a teeny pair of
clogs on a tiny little truck. "People have been
wearing clogs in Holland for centuries," Dirk

explained as he handed Jake the clogs. "We call them *klompen*," he said.

Jake and Katie laughed again. "Clogs look like *klompen*. The word fits them," Katie said.

Later they got off the train at Rotterdam by the sea.

There were ships everywhere, many as big as a huge building. Big cranes lifted huge containers of cargo off some ships and loaded containers onto others. Katie and Jake had never seen so many huge ships in one place. Dirk said it was once the biggest harbor in the world.

Unless the bikes were moving, Cooper became restless in the basket, so they continued to ride past the huge ships and big, clean storage buildings. After their bike tour of Rotterdam, they got back on board the train again.

This time they got off at Scheveningen, a sandy beach that stretched for miles.

"Look at that sign," Jake pointed out. It said 4 kilometers.

"A kilometer is about a half-mile. I bet you don't know how long a mile is." Dirk challenged Jake.

"I do so! It's 20 city street blocks!" Jake declared.

There were colorful pavilions along the beach that sold all kinds of food. Each one was different. That's what made it so pretty. There were flocks of birds everywhere.

Cooper ran free. They took off their shoes and ran with him on the edge of the water. He kept trying to catch a seagull, but the birds always outsmarted him.

Tired, Cooper ran up to them. He shook himself off, sprinkling them with water while they squealed, partly annoyed and partly amused. They were all tired, so they nestled together and took a short nap in the sun.

When they woke up, they were hungry again.

"This time we'll try *pannenkoeken*," said Dirk as they walked inside a small restaurant where they split a treat of pancakes with ham, cheese and tomato on top. It didn't sound like they'd like it. But they did. Cooper must have been hungry again, too, because even he ate the tomato Jake gave him.

"Did the *pannenkoeken* count for lunch?" Jake wondered. He liked eating whenever he wanted.

Now that they'd seen the seaside, they decided to visit the downtown part of The Hague. The Hague is the home of the Dutch government, and the buildings all look very official. They couldn't possibly see everything there—like Parliament and the queen's palace—in so little time. They had to pick one place they'd most like to see.

Katie wanted to see the queen's palace. She wanted to know what it would be like to be a queen and live in the palace, but she was outvoted by Jake and Dirk who wanted to go to Gevangenpoort.

"Gevangenpoort?" asked Katie.

"It's a cool place. It's a famous prison where people were tortured, but now it's a museum," said Dirk.

"Yeah," said Jake. "Let's go."

They read a sign: See a collection of medieval instruments of torture. This prison was built in 1296.

"Long before anything was built in your country," Dirk said proudly.

They walked past a cell that once held hundreds of people. According to the sign, the cell was so crowded the prisoners couldn't even sit down. All they had to eat was a little bread and water.

"Boy, they could have used a secret cover

here," said Jake. He couldn't take his eyes off the noose.

Jake didn't want to leave, but Dirk coaxed him: "Want to try *kibberling*?"

"What's that?" asked Jake as they left the prison. Jake hoped it was a game, but *kibberling* was fish that was fried.

Fish wasn't their favorite food, but this fish was fried in a delicious batter, and the little bite they took did not taste fishy at all. In fact, it was pretty yummy, so Dirk bought *kibberling* for each of them. Cooper seemed to like it, too.

CHAPTER EIGHT

Cooper's Gone!

I T WAS THE MOST fun-filled day Katie and
Jake thought they'd ever spent, but they were
glad to return to Amsterdam. It was getting
late, and Dirk knew he had better get home.

They got off the train. Katie put her backpack
in her basket once again. Then Dirk reached down
to pick up Cooper. Cooper was gone.

"Cooper!" Katie called, looking around franti-
cally. "Cooper!!" they all shouted. They looked up,
down and across the street. No Cooper. "He'd been
so good about staying with us," she said anxiously.

Dirk held Katie by the shoulders. "Try not to
panic. People are very good to dogs in Holland. If
Cooper's gone, someone will help him. They'll
take him to the humane society."

"What's a humane society?" Jake asked.

"It's a place where people take dogs they find,
dogs that don't have a home," Dirk explained.

Katie knew there was no use standing there.
Cooper was gone, and he wouldn't come back until
he was ready to be found. But they couldn't just

stand there all night.

Dirk made a phone call. "My dad said I have to be home by 6:30 and no later," he said.

They got on their bikes and rode up and down the streets calling for Cooper. Although Katie was sad about Cooper, she couldn't help thinking that everything looked magical as the sun set.

Each bicycle had its own light, so they could continue to look for Cooper. All they had to do was push a lever to bring a round gear next to the wheel. As the wheel turned, the gear did, too. That

Cooper was gone. The kids got on their bikes and rode up and down the streets searching for their lost dog.

generated just enough electricity to light their way as they rode their bikes. When they stopped, the lights dimmed.

They'd been looking for Cooper for over an hour. Dirk said he'd have to go home and suggested they come with him.

Home? Katie thought about her room in the apartment in New York City, where everything was familiar. She thought about Aunt Jean's farm and the sound of crickets and the smell of sweet summer air. Her heart felt heavy.

Slowly and silently Dirk, Katie and Jake
pedaled along the streets. Tired from pedaling all
day, they got off their bikes and walked on the
sidewalk.

Jake looked through the windows of the shops
and restaurants along the way. He was really tired
of walking and looking. He asked Katie if he
could wear the glasses. He stopped in front of a
shop window and put them on.

They made him look funny, but since they
didn't hurt his eyes, he decided to wear them for
a while. He tried to see his reflection in the
windows as he passed by. That took his mind off
Cooper—at least for a little while–as they walked
down even more streets.

"I'll find him eventually, even if it's after you
go," Dirk offered, knowing that wasn't enough to
make them feel better. He added, "I'll never stop
looking for him."

"Wait… Katie look!" yelled Jake.

He took off his glasses and put them back on
again. Then he gave them to Katie.

Purple paw tracks! She could see purple paw
tracks with the glasses on—nothing with them off.
So they began tracking Cooper, over bridges,
along the waterway, through alleyways. They

couldn't believe how much territory Cooper had covered. Where would they find him? Who would he be with? Was he in danger?

Finally, the tracks led them to a beautiful canal house with lace curtains in the front windows and window boxes filled with flowers.

"The prints come up here and go out again," said Katie. They rang the doorbell. There was nobody home.

"I know this house. It belongs to Madame van den Berg. She used to sew for my uncle. My uncle said she was very wealthy. Sometimes she didn't want to take money for the work she did. She just wanted to be busy."

"Maybe Cooper came here because of the scarf!" Katie yelled. The trunk's advice and Aunt Jean's farm felt very long ago and very far away.

Again, they rang the bell. No answer.

They followed the prints back down to the curb. That was it. No more prints.

"Maybe he got hit by a car in the street," said Katie sadly. She had been so happy that they would finally find Cooper. Now she was feeling let down.

Dirk, Katie and Jake pedaled along the streets again. It was late, and Dirk said they really must go home. They started walking toward Dirk's house, when Katie saw paw prints again. This time they were coming from the curb and led right into a fancy restaurant. They ran to the window and peeked inside.

White table cloths. Candles. Shiny silverware. Big, round white plates with gold rims. They also saw Cooper on a chair finishing off what looked like a very full meal. He was seated across from an old woman dressed in black.

Jake jumped up and down while tapping on the window to get Cooper's attention. Cooper was too busy eating to notice.

A waiter in a dark suit with a white shirt and tie emerged from the restaurant to shoo them away. "That's OUR dog!!!" Jake declared, pointing toward Cooper and marching toward the restaurant door.

"Young man, Madame is patronizing our establishment and will not be interrupted by you! Now run along," and with that he put his sizable body in front of the door.

Jake shouted, causing the waiter to turn on his heel and close the door—hard.

They walked their bikes across the street and watched from a distance, imagining all the food

Cooper wriggled out of the waiter's arms and tore off down the street. Katie, Jake and Dirk saw Cooper had cornered a black cat in a doorway.

Cooper was eating. "We'll get him when they come out," Katie said.

"He doesn't look like he missed us much," Jake said.

After a few moments, the door opened and Cooper emerged in the arms of the waiter with the old woman by his side. They spoke in Dutch. Dirk whispered a translation.

"Good evening, Madame van den Berg. It was a pleasure to see you this evening. It has been entirely too long," said the waiter.

Madame van den Berg stretched a hand toward Cooper. "Why thank you. It was nice to be here. I loved having company for dinner. Rom was a perfect gentleman," she said, reaching to pet Cooper.

"Rom? That's not his name!" Jake protested.

"She doesn't know that," Katie said.

"She stole our dog!" yelled Jake.

"Sshhh!!!" Katie and Dirk said simultaneously.

Madame van den Berg continued to chat with the waiter as a cab pulled up.

"We better say something now," Katie said as she moved forward.

Cooper didn't seem to like being held by the waiter. He turned this way and that. Finally

Cooper wriggled out of the waiter's arms and tore off down the street. Katie, Jake and Dirk saw he had cornered a black cat in a doorway. Cooper barked, without any regard to anyone or anything else.

"Cooper!!!! Stop right now!" yelled both Katie and Jake.

Much to their amazement, Cooper actually stopped barking. His ears perked up. He listened and charged back toward Katie and Jake.

Jump and lick for Katie. Jump and lick for Jake. They were all overjoyed until the long-suited arm of the waiter snatched Cooper away from them.

Cooper squirmed, but that only made the waiter hold him tighter. No one in his life had ever mistreated him in any way. Even when he was a pest, he just got scolded.

Cooper growled, showed his teeth and then nipped the waiter right at the end of his nose. "That dog is a menace!" the waiter hissed to Madame van den Berg as he patted his nose with his handkerchief.

Then he abruptly turned on his heel and headed back to the restaurant.

Katie, Jake and Dirk kept their distance from

Madame van den Berg, but they didn't want to just run away from her. "I...I mean, we...we would like to thank you," Katie stammered, "for taking care of Cooper."

The cab driver was entertained by the spectacle, but now seemed eager to go.

Madame van den Berg regarded them closely. "My word, you all look tired. Why don't you lock your bikes here, and let me have the driver take you home."

"But we can't come with you. You're a stranger!" warned Jake.

"No she's not," said Dirk. "I know her from when she sewed for my Uncle Peter."

"Oh, so you are Peter van Dyke's nephew. Oh my, that was many years ago—when these stiff old fingers worked better," she laughed. "Then you'll come with me?"

"Yes!" yelled Jake, who was tired, hungry and glad to be with a grown-up.

The restaurant was empty of guests when the waiter returned. The cashier and the other waiters were counting out the money they'd made in tips for the day. "Look at you, Dan! That small dog got the best of you." They laughed as they pointed at his nose.

The waiter's face turned red, more from anger than embarrassment.

"Laugh all you want," he said as he reached into his pocket. "It is I who got the best of them all!" and he pulled out the purple collar that Cooper had worn around his neck.

The waiters took turns holding the collar. "It must be worth a lot of money," said the waiter. "Maybe I'll sell it or return it to her for a handsome reward!"

The waiter dreamed about his good fortune and how much Madame van den Berg would pay.

CHAPTER NINE

The Madame and Great-Grandpa

IN THE CAB, Madame van den Berg asked Katie and Jake where they were from. She knew by their accent that they were American.

"Where are your parents staying?" she asked.

"They're in Mexico," said Jake.

"Katie and Jake are visiting Holland and staying with me while their folks are away," said Dirk. "They're here to learn about Holland." At least that wasn't a lie, Katie thought. They did come to learn about Holland.

"And how long have you been here?" asked Madame van den Berg.

"A few hours," said Jake.

"Do your parents know you'll be having guests tonight?" Madame van den Berg asked Dirk.

"It's just my dad, and he won't mind," said Dirk.

Madame van den Berg suggested that maybe Katie and Jake could come home with her, and Dirk could come by for them in the morning. Katie and Jake liked the idea of staying with this

Lia brought out a tray with stacks and stacks of plates filled with all sorts of food.

woman who made friends with Cooper. Everybody was in agreement.

After dropping off Dirk, the cab driver brought them to the door of the very same house where the prints had led them.

The house was filled with stuff, more clutter than they'd ever seen in their lives, but it wasn't junk clutter—it was lots of very unusual things. There were rugs on every floor and even a small one on a side table. China was displayed in glass closets, and there were paintings everywhere.

Katie and Jake would have to be careful not to break things here.

"You must be starving," said Madame van den Berg. "I'll bet you haven't eaten all day." Jake was about to tell her all the new things he'd eaten, but he didn't have a chance. Within moments they were escorted to the dining room, and a maid appeared with a tray of cheese and crackers.

"Lia, say hello to Katie and Jake," said Madame van den Berg.

Kate and Jake nodded hello as Lia shook their hands.

"I've asked Lia to bring in some cheese. A lot of cheese is made in Holland," Madame van den Berg explained. "See this round one in the red wrapper? Years ago during a sea battle they'd run out of cannon balls so they used their cargo of cheese instead."

Jake took a piece. It wasn't every day he had a chance to eat food that could be used as ammunition.

Lia set the table. In front of them sat bowls filled with hot green soup with cubes of toasted bread and sliced sausages on top.

Katie and Jake stared at it. "It's pea soup. The Dutch word is *snert*," said Madame van den Berg.

"*Snert?*" said Katie and Jake together. They tried not to laugh. They didn't want to seem impolite.

Katie dipped her spoon into the soup and sipped it. It tasted better than it sounded. Jake fished out a few sausages but was reluctant to go back for more.

Lia brought out a tray with stacks and stacks of plates filled with all sorts of food. Madame van den Berg called it Indonesian Rijsttafel. It sounded like she was saying "rice taffel." She said it meant "rice table."

As Lia served the food, it was clear why it was called a rice table: The table was covered with dishes—a large main rice dish and smaller plates.

Some plates had spices to put on the rice. Others had coconut that added a sweet taste. Katie and Jake liked the coconut best.

After the dinner plates were cleaned off, Lia placed a beautiful gold box on the table that was filled with chocolate for dessert.

When they finished dinner, Katie and Jake followed Madame van den Berg into the parlor. She stroked Cooper, who hadn't thought a thing about jumping up on the elegant sofa.

They could barely stay awake as Madame van den Berg described how excited she was when she saw Cooper at her doorstep, barking as though he had a delivery for her.

Suddenly Katie felt wide awake. The scarf! Did Cooper try to find her? Katie pulled out the scarf in her backpack and took it to Madame van den Berg.

She held it in her bony hands and looked at Katie and Jake for a long, long time. "He promised he'd come back to me, and I promised I'd never forget him," said Madame van den Berg.

Jake felt the dog tags around his neck get warm. She didn't have to explain that she was talking about Great-Grandpa Henry. Jake knew.

"During World War II, I was a seamstress. I

made uniforms for the soldiers, and I washed and mended clothes for those who were wounded.

That's where I met Henry Anderson. He'd been hurt when his plane was shot down, but he didn't stay in the hospital long…just long enough for me to get to know him and remember him for the rest of my life."

"Great-Grandpa Henry was our great grandfather, but we never knew him," said Jake. "He died a long time ago." Katie wished Jake hadn't blurted it out like that.

"He was 29 and I was just 18 when the American troops landed in Holland," said Madame van den Berg. "I was afraid he'd be gone from the world by now."

"I have his dog tags," said Jake, and he pulled them out. Both Katie and Jake began telling her all about Great-Grandpa Henry's trunk.

"I have something for you both," she said, as she interrupted them. She opened a carved wooden box. Inside was a purple medal on a ribbon and a purple bracelet.

"You were an Undercover Kid?" Katie asked.

"I wanted to go everywhere and do everything when I was young like you. I used my bracelet to go to Africa and India…Malaysia, too," she said.

"What about the medal?" asked Jake.

"Your great-grandfather sent it to me years after the war. Will you take it and keep it always?" she asked as she handed it to Katie. "I knew when I saw Cooper's collar that Henry was saying hello…or goodbye."

Hearing his name, Cooper's ears perked up. That's when Jake noticed that Cooper's collar was gone!

"I last saw it in the restaurant," Madame said.

The restaurant? The waiter! Katie and Jake thought that the mean waiter must be involved with the lost collar. "He stole the collar!" yelled Jake. The trunk had warned them about people who would be jealous of the bands.

"What happens if he keeps it?" asked Katie.

"The bracelets are a circle of power connecting Undercover Kids everywhere. When bracelets are lost or stolen the circle is broken. Eventually, travel stops," Madame explained. "We'll find it tomorrow. Don't worry," she said calmly.

Katie and Jake felt that Madame van den Berg was as worried about losing Cooper's collar as they were.

Lia led Katie and Jake upstairs to their room. She asked that they leave their dirty clothes outside their room, and she gave them towels to wrap themselves in.

They slipped into their beds and felt the crisp, cool sheets next to their bare skin. Soon the beds were warm from their own body heat, and they slept.

Jake had no idea what time it was or how long he had slept. All he knew for sure was that it was dark, and he had a great idea. He grabbed his towel and tip-toed out the door and down the stairs.

He saw Madame van den Berg sipping tea in the parlor and petting Cooper.

"Madame van den Berg," Jake said quietly.

Madame van den Berg was startled. "Why Jake, can't you sleep?"

"I was dreaming about losing Cooper's collar," said Jake. "I wanted to fight that waiter, but he was bigger than me. So I though up a plan, and in my dream I found the collar."

"Do you want to tell me about it?" asked Madame van den Berg.

CHAPTER TEN

The Purple Ribbon Solution

IT WAS MORNING when they were awakened by a loud knock on the downstairs door. It was Dirk. They heard Madame van den Berg speaking with him in Dutch. Wrapped in her towel, Katie opened the door a sliver to listen. She saw their freshly laundered clothes neatly piled outside.

Jake dressed quickly and ran down the stairs with Katie following behind. Dirk smiled as he told Katie about Jake and Madame van den Berg's plan.

Madame van den Berg asked Lia to call a cab. They all got inside and made room for three large, filled baskets.

She asked the cab driver to drop them off a block before the restaurant. They all got out and took the baskets from the cab and went to work.

From inside the baskets, they pulled out purple ribbons that looked just like Cooper's collar. Unless you held one, you wouldn't know it was different from the real collar. They gave every single dog they saw a purple ribbon collar, and they put one on Cooper as well. Everyone was happy to be given such a beautiful collar...for free.

Jake was excited to have thought up the plan. He pulled on Madame van den Berg's sleeve, and she bent down slowly to listen. "Sometimes it's better to have a plan than to start a fight," he whispered.

When at least 20 dogs had new collars, Dirk, Katie, Jake and Madame van den Berg locked arms and walked toward the restaurant.

One waiter, looking out the window, saw the four of them approach. He called to the others inside.

"Why Madame van den Berg," said the waiter, feeling the stolen collar in his pocket. Looking around he wondered why the other waiters were laughing. Were they jealous of the fortune that was about to come his way?

The waiter looked up to see all the waiters pointing to Cooper's collar and then to all the other collars they saw on the street. "Your collar is oh so very valuable," one waiter whispered in his ear. "She's bound to give you a huge reward," laughed another.

Madame van den Berg pretended nothing was

*They gave every single dog they saw
a purple ribbon collar, and they put
one on Cooper as well.*

wrong as she asked about the dinner specials. The waiter mentioned a few of the items, and then at last he said, "Look what I found on the street. I saved it for you." He felt foolish. The collar was so common. There would be no reward. His hopes were gone.

Madame van den Berg looked at it. "Oh, did we drop that silly collar? My, it's rather dirty. I can't imagine any use for it now, but since you went to so much trouble, why thank you." She took the collar from him and turned to walk away.

"Will you be dining here this evening?" asked the waiter. Cooper looked at the waiter and growled.

"Not this evening," said Madame van den Berg with a forced smile. She vowed she would never eat in that restaurant again.

"The TIME!" Katie yelled as she glanced at the church clock. She didn't realize they were so late. They put Cooper in Dirk's basket, tied his collar on him and turned to Madame van den Berg.

"We had better get you something for the trip," she said as she led them across the street to a candy store. "You'll love these salty licorice candies…they're called drops. And look, you can pick out a chocolate letter for the first letter of your name. There's a K...and there's a J."

"What about Cooper?" asked Jake.

"Chocolate isn't good for dogs. Besides, Cooper's had enough," Katie exclaimed as she patted Cooper's plump belly.

The cab pulled up to the curb. Madame van den Berg touched the dog tags that Jake wore on his neck. "You did a very good deed by visiting me," she said.

"But we didn't do a good deed," Jake insisted. "All we did was find Cooper and take him away from you."

"Sometimes you can do good deeds without even realizing it," said Madame van den Berg.

"You can?" asked Jake, amazed that it could be so easy to be so good.

"Besides, he is a rambunctious dog with too much energy for an old woman like me. But I loved his company." A sad look passed over her face. "I believe my dog days are over."

"I know where there's a dog for you," said Jake. "The humane society." So much had happened that Katie had forgotten about the humane society.

Madame van den Berg reached for Jake and hugged him for a moment. Then she pulled Katie close and hugged her too. She stepped back as she said goodbye.

"The humane society," she instructed the cab driver, giving Katie and Jake a wink as the cab pulled away.

Anne Frank's Museum was closed as they rode up on their bicycles, just as it had been when they arrived. "How will you get the bikes back?" Katie asked Dirk.

"I leave them here for other Undercover Kids," he said. Katie nodded.

"Do a lot come over?" Katie asked.

Dirk smiled. "We have so much we never spoke of. Just remember, the more you travel, the more you'll learn." Dirk touched his bracelet on the front door, and it swung open.

Katie lifted Cooper out of the basket. She opened her backpack to put the candy inside when the picture she had taken from the trunk fell out into her bike basket.

She'd never really looked at it closely before. Gently she held it up. Even though the years had faded the image, she saw the picture of a beautiful woman in a jacket with big shoulders. She had dark and wavy hair, sparkling eyes and a broad smile.

Katie looked at the photo and saw it was signed "Anna." Because the ink was smudged, it was hard to read the full name. Katie could see a 'V' but nothing more.

"Anna is Madame van den Berg," said Katie. "I just know it."

Dirk laughed. "We don't know her first name and practically everyone in Holland has a last name that starts with a 'V.' You see, 'van' in Dutch means from. Van den Berg means from the mountain. Van Stadt means from the city. Van der Tuin means from the garden. Long ago, those families came from those places."

Katie knew that the picture should go to Madame van den Berg. "Please return this to her, Dirk, would you?" asked Katie as she handed him the framed photo.

"I will," said Dirk. "I promise to give this to

her and visit her often, too."

Slowly, the three children climbed the stairs.

"Now, you understand about the trip back? You'll have the power to go back to yesterday at exactly the time you left. No one will ever know you've gone, unless, of course, you tell them."

"I want to know so much more about you, the Undercover Kids and Holland," Katie exclaimed.

"That's what it means to be an Undercover Kid," said Dirk. "You want to know more about other places and other people. And the more you know, the more you'll want to know...and the more you'll understand."

And with that, he opened the cover. They stepped inside. Dirk gave Jake a big thumbs-up and he looked at Katie in a way that made her happy to have made a friend, but she felt awkward because she didn't know what to say.

CHAPTER ELEVEN

Home Again

I N AN INSTANT, they were being pulled along once again. They traveled faster than they could think. They passed pictures of Holland— places they had seen and places they hadn't. They saw beautiful artwork, windmills and a giant dam holding back the sea.

This time, Katie noticed there were turnoffs everywhere with signs that must lead to other places: Siberia. Belize. Argentina. Canada.

Just as she was beginning to enjoy the speed, the trip was over. They opened the cover and climbed out.

Katie took off Cooper's collar. She dropped her bracelet and Jake's into her backpack. Cooper jumped out and started running around in circles as Katie and Jake emerged. They put the cover on tight and threw a few branches and stones on top.

They walked slowly up the path to the house and heard Aunt Jean and her friends chatting away. The sound of Aunt Jean's voice and the sight of the farmhouse made Katie and Jake realize how happy they were to be home.

Inside, over milk and cookies, they listened as

"Ah-hem," Katie said to the trunk.
When she got no response she reached
for the trunk lid.

the women laughed and chatted.

Katie and Jake were exhausted. Although they could barely keep their eyes open through dinner, they managed to stay awake until Aunt Jean's friends left. They said goodnight when they finished and walked upstairs.

Katie felt oddly alone in her own room, but it wasn't long before Jake tiptoed in. They didn't have to worry about Cooper. He'd fallen asleep by the kitchen table.

Katie wouldn't let Jake go to asleep. She nudged him every time his eyes started drooping. She asked him to remember everything he possibly could about Holland. Finally, she heard Aunt Jean's bedroom door close.

Once they felt sure that Aunt Jean was asleep, Katie reached for the backpack. She and Jake tiptoed up to the attic. Jake stepped on the trunk and pulled the string for the light. The trunk rumbled then settled back down, as though it too had been asleep.

"Ah-hem," Katie said. When they got no response, Katie reached for the trunk lid.

"Jumping Jehosaphat!!!"

The trunk rose up in the air and flipped open and shut. "Don't sneak up on me like that. You could scare an old trunk like me half to death."

"We didn't mean to scare you," said Katie, finding it very strange that a trunk that stayed up in an attic like this would be frightened of anything. "We just wanted to put back our bracelets. And this medal. It's for you."

The trunk was very quiet. "And here are some clogs for you too," said Jake, putting the clogs Dirk had given him in the trunk as well.

"Until another day," said Katie.

"Until another day?" said the trunk. "That's it? No news? No telling about what happened? Just three words? What's the matter? Don't you trust me to keep a lid on things?"

"Did we upset you?" Katie asked. "We know we can trust you. It's just that..."

> *Don't you worry, I won't say a word.*
> *You never told me and I never heard*
> *How you traveled to Holland across*
>   *the sea,*
> *Met Dirk, lost Cooper and helped*
>   *Anna vdB*

"Then you know... everything?" Katie asked.

"We trunks don't like being kept in the dark," the trunk said.

As they turned off the light and climbed down

the attic stairs, they heard the trunk's laugh echo softly through the attic.

Both Katie and Jake fell asleep in Katie's bed at last.

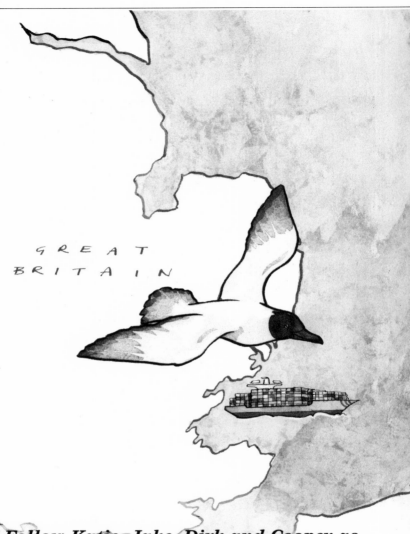

GREAT BRITAIN

Follow Katie, Jake, Dirk and Cooper as they bicycle through Holland. They enjoy great food, have fun on the beach and meet their Great-Grandpa's friend, Madame van den Berg.

Madurodam
The Hague

Scheveningen
Amsterdam
.
The Hague
Rotterdam

Gevangenpoort
The Hague

GERMANY

BELGIUM

SHORT STORY CONTEST

Write your own Undercover Kids' Adventure

If you would like to become a published writer, here's your chance! Make up your own story featuring Katie, Jake and Cooper, and it might be published in the next Undercover Kids' Adventure book or on the web.

Where do you want to take Katie, Jake and Cooper? Would you like them to travel to one of your favorite places? They may visit your hometown or a faraway land. You choose.

Visit **TheUndercoverKids.com**

Here's What To Do...

- Be creative!
- Entries must be 500 words or less
- Open to all kids between the ages of 8-12
- Give your story a title

If your story is picked to be included in the next Undercover Kids' Adventure book you will receive a prize of $50.00 and an official Undercover Kids certificate recognizing that you are a published author. All submissions will be published online.

All entries will require written permission by a parent or guardian before being published. One winner will be chosen for the next Undercover Kids' Adventure book from each age group: 8-9 year olds and 10-12 year olds.

Mail your entries to:

The Undercover Kids
174 South Street
Newburgh, NY 12550

Be sure to include your name, address, and phone number so that if you're chosen as a winner we can contact you to give you your prize!

for more excitement and fun.

 Author Gloria Smith Zawaski grew up as a tomboy and never lost her love of westerns, the outdoors and horses. Gloria is mom to two boys. She and her husband Alex live in Middletown, New York. They have flown a single engine plane everywhere. Her Springer Spaniel, Bailey, has slowed down a bit over the years, but not very long ago he bore a resemblance to Cooper.

 Karen Donnelly has turned a childhood love of reading and drawing into a career. Over the years she has worked on all sorts of contemporary and classic fiction and nonfiction for children and adults. Karen lives by the sea in the South of England, with her husband and three children. She works in an untidy attic with noisy seagulls on the roof for company.

**To become a Community Partner,
go to www.TheUndercoverKids.com**

- Complete the Community Partner form
- You will be assigned a code to be used when ordering books online
- We provide the flyer that announces the book promotion
- Order books online using your code
- Begin earning money for your community projects

Our Undercover Kids' series promotes peace and tolerance by helping kids develop an understanding of how kids in other cultures live. Become part of The Undercover Kids Adventure. Raise money for your programs and services now.

Earn money for your organization.